One Cold Kiss

by

Joe Campbell

'Sing to me of the man... The man of twists and turns.'

The Odyssey: Homer.

'Tell me where your hurting ends and where your fear begins...'

'Open' by Joe Campbell

For Brigid, Emma, Sarah and
my Mother

BEGINNING:

I had the dreams again…

Including the one where I'm running down that grim corridor, can't stop. For, like some great bear, he's relentless, unceasing, in pursuit.

Then, I'm at the window. The high, arch window. My fingers press cool, damp, glass as the city, like diamonds on velvet, twinkles up at me.

And that's when I see him.

Him and his walrus moustache and his uniform cap and his yellow oilskins dripping rainwater.

'Why?' I mumble, as he points his service revolver, smiles.

If you could call it that?

I hear the hammer being thumbed, see his index finger twitch, when… Bang! I get slammed back, hard.

They say when you get shot, shock delays the pain.

It's not true!

As I look down, see that hole in my chest, I hear sounds like someone breaking eggs. For the bullet, having passed clean through, has shattered the window. Then, as a rush of wind buffets me, I gasp; for I'm now falling backwards through a hail-storm of glass.

And, as the city swoops up to greet me, I think…

One

You can't dream your own death. Can you?

Meanwhile, and with a pain that pins my head to the pillow, the 'Hangover Express' shunts into the station.

'Unh!' I try to sit, notice the bedroom window swings wide and I'm still in my day clothes, dark jeans and shirt. I fumble for a cigarette, light up, cough. On my feet, trying to stifle the cough

I don't want to disturb Jess.

I drop the cigarette, forgetting I'm barefoot. 'Aow!' I stamp it out. Investigating my injury one arm props me against the window-sill. It slips. As a red vase gets upended I snatch at air, watch helplessly as it hits the floor, pulverizes.

For a moment, all is still...

When, accompanied by a frenzy of activity, the door, its handle indenting the wall gets flung open. And there, in black trousers and oyster blouse, I see her,

My lovely Jess.

phone and devil key-ring in one hand, shiny black sling backs in the other.

'Anybody there? If that's you? I- I'll…' she's anxious, her voice has that odd, heightened, quality.

Pursing soft full lips, she enters the room when

With those big brown eyes of hers.

she sees the shattered remnants of the vase.

'You better not be in here, playing tricks on me.' applying clips to long, crow-black hair.

But I'm already under the bed, behind the lip of the quilt, shaking my head as if to say, 'No. I'm not here.' as, just for the moment, I'd prefer she didn't see the shattered remnants of me.

Toeing the remains of the vase into a neat pile, she closes the window, and I smell her scent.

Her warm lingering scent.

Pulling on a shoe, a strap gets caught in a flared trouser-end, I want to tell her, but think the better of it. Taking a jacket from behind the door, about to go, she slips it on.

Hurray!

She pauses.

Oh no!

She senses something.

Oh no. No. No!

Her knees bend.

Please don't. Not under the bed!

Can't move. I'm paralyzed.

What to do?

A corner of the quilt slowly rises.

I can't let her find me…

And rises.

Not like this!

When…

``Bleep-bleep-bleep``, she looks to her phone, turns, and is gone.

As her heels click-clack their way downstairs, I wait for the front door to close then, dragging myself from under the bed, I lie there until the searing pain becomes a dull, dismal throb and that faint, snapping, noise inside my head stops.

I need a shower!

Before I know it, I'm in the cubicle, head against cool tiles. As the needle-fine water hits I grope blindly for gel, find one marked 'Revitalizing', discover it isn't. Then, sliding to the shower floor, for some strange reason I start to cry.

Two

Having raided the wardrobe, found some loose-fitting clothes,

Have I lost weight?

I go downstairs. Flies buzz a table topped by beer bottles and cardboard wine containers while smoked butts form a pyramid in an overfull ashtray.

Was I...? Did I...? I don't remember.

As staleness pervades, my stomach heaves. From the corner, an old C.D. player whirrs, pauses, whirrs again. I wish it'd stop for my head still throbs. I go to the kitchen pour milk, take painkillers. Coming back in I slump into the armchair, sit on the remote. The music plays mid-song...

``Tell me when your hurting ends and where your fear begins... ``

Meanwhile, as I take another sip of milk, I note the analgesia begin to have an almost immediate effect. And then, as my eyelids seem to grow heav-

I find I'm in a clearing in the middle of a forest. And it's dark. A murky, impenetrable dark. As a thick fog billows in I blink, for it seems to sting my eyes. I hear noise, comforting at first, like rain drumming on tin. As the noise gets nearer, it gets louder. Then I see Jess and, as she reaches out to me, I can tell she's anxious. The fog, meanwhile, billows all around her. When, in an instant, she disappears inside it. The noise now thunderous, almost bursting my eardrums, I find I'm on my knees.

'Enough!' I roar. And that's when the noise changes…

To the phone's persistent bleating. Disoriented I stumble from the chair, slip on the now spilled milk. By the time I get to my feet the phone has stopped. Catching my breath, I notice the phone rests on a book called 'Emotional Intelligence.'

I should read that.

It rings again.

'Hehwo?' my tongue stuck to the roof of my mouth.

'Is Jess there?' a rasping voice, in the background I hear the familiar, eerie strains of…

Oh, what is it?

'No, she's... Who's thi...?'

He hangs up.

It rings again. I put it to my ear, only the dislocated eeriness of,

Got it, 'Gnossienne No.1' by Satie.

When, just then, that image fills my head…

A bald man, no eyebrows, he wears a green paisley dressing gown. His head and face are scarred, thickly powdered white. As he moves little plumes of powder spiral upward when… Click, he hangs up again and I, victim of an overactive imagination, shudder.

Meanwhile, phone in hand, its ``**Brr**``, buzzing in my ear, I look at it as if it's going to give me answers. It doesn't. I decide to ring Jess at work, can't remember the number. I scroll the phone memory, see 'Jess-Work', press the button. It rings three times, the tone pleasing, reassuring.

'Hello, 'Harbinger and Associates'. How may I help you?' A singsong voice, girlish.

Such a sweet voice.

'Harbinger and Associates. How may I help you?' impatience seeps through as I keep her waiting longer than comfortable.

'Sorry, could I speak to Jess, please.'

Maybe I'm overreacting.

'Is that business or personal?'

'Personal.' I say.

'Oh, is that Justin?' gleefully.

'No!' I reel. I'm about to ask who Justin is, when…

'I'm sorry Miss Grimason is not in work today. Thank you for calling Harbinger and Associates. Goodbye!' her, now matter-of-fact, tone failing to mask her unease, she hangs up.

And I'm left with that, ``Brr!`` again. I decide to ring Jess's mobile, the name 'Justin' reverberating like a car alarm. I scroll again, press the button marked 'Jess'; a tinny voice of indeterminate gender responds.

``I'm sorry but the person you are calling cannot take your call...``

I hang up, again my stomach heaves, again I hyperventilate.

I need air!

I stumble outside, still parked, I spy Jess' Mini Cooper, managing a, 'But how?' I get in, immediately notice her little devil keyring swaying in the ignition. In quiet panic, I pull closed the door, see her phone on its side on the passenger seat.

She would never… Could never… Not without her phone.

I turn it over. Its sealed envelope symbol displays '4 missed calls'. I decide to find out who the calls are from. Using the retrieval number, I get another tinny voice.

``You have four new messages…``

I play each message, my shock only subsides at the end of the fourth, for it, like the previous three, comprises solely of a snatch of the 'Gnossienne'. I throw the phone down, pummel my head against the headrest. The name 'Justin' still reverberates, now less like a car alarm, more like notes from a badly tuned piano.

Through the windscreen I see I've drawn the attention of a woman I feel I should recognize but can't quite place. She wears a floral print dress, pink novelty slippers. She places a bowl of milk in front of a black cat who sidles against her, flicks her with his tail.

Least I assume it's a, he.

As I acknowledge her with a wave and a smile, she raises a pointy chin, that juts below those crimson lips of hers, gives me a look that's strangely forlorn. Meanwhile, trying to act casual, I turn the engine over, select reverse, ease into the road. I wave to her again. She's still gives me that look, when it occurs to me…

I haven't an inkling as to where I'm going.

Three

Passing row after row of garish, identikit houses, the weather changes. Gone the sharp clear morning; in its place, a rolling bank of charcoal cloud. And then it starts to rain.

Not just any rain…

No, this rain tumbles down in greasy droplets that sluice across the windscreen, the wipers on full scarcely able to cope.

Finally, I'm into the grey, gridlock suburbia. My knuckles show white as I grip the steering wheel tight, snarled up, as I now am, behind a funeral cortege, at the head of which an antiquated hearse barely moves, but at least he's going somewhere.

I say 'he' for Father is spelled out in floral tribute.

Meanwhile what must be just minutes seem to take an eternity to pass.

And no, the irony isn't lost on me.

I turn on the radio, scan. Nothing but Techno-beats, bile inducing boy bands and Death Metal Thrash presided over by self-regarding deejays with their ``Comin'atchas!`` and their ``This one's for you…`` I find the classical station, am immediately transported by 'The Flower Duet' from 'Lakme' by Delibes, only for it to crackle out, get replaced by, surely a coincidence, that 'Gnossienne'. Nonetheless I'm now locked onto the station and all I can get is Satie. Becoming

Uncharacteristically.

enraged I give a blast on the car horn. When…

Oh no!

from the rear window of an antique funeral car, three serene faces, framed in white, turn to look at me. It's only when, rosary beads in hand, they make the sign of the cross at me, that I see they're nuns. In return, not only do I smile, I hold it far too long when, as a lick of lightning flicks across the sky, the cortege begins to move, their car peels away and

Thankfully.

they're gone.

Looming into view, on my left, I see the dark old, ramshackle police station, the one with the

'Police' sign that flickers. When, just then, the chatter starts…

Should I go in? And what? Report Jess missing! Is she missing? Course she is! Then what? Tell them about Justin! Tell them what about Justin?... Maybe best not to.

I flick a mental coin. It comes up heads. I pull in. Leaving the 'hazards' on I cut the engine. Then, jacket over head, I get out and think…

Is this my jacket? Or, is it Justin's? Maybe, that's why it doesn't fit?... Lose weight indeed!

Rain spatters, as I run up the steps of the Masonic symbolled porch where I shake the jacket out just as a young, grim faced, officer brusquely brushes past.

'Bad day for it!' he announces, splashing toward a patrol car.

'Bad day for what exactly?' I'm tempted to shout, but instead mutter it under my breath.

Pushing through reluctant swing doors I enter a foyer, with grubby green vinyl flooring, where church pews for seating await. And where a reinforced glass arch sits fixed to a wooden counter top. I'm about to press what looks like a doorbell when…

'No!' I reel. For just now, 'No, couldn't be!'

That same bear of a policeman

With the walrus moustache!?

has just come through a door behind. I reassure myself,

Just a coincidence.

console myself he's not carrying a gun.

Even so, after the day I've had.

All I can do is divert my focus elsewhere, which is when I notice he carries papers, that he tosses to one side.

With his, ahem, 'bearlike' paw.

As he lumbers toward the arch, a bulging shirt does it's best to contain an impressive stomach, while a radio mouthpiece, attached to an epaulette, crackles as he walks. Then, elbows down, he leans on the counter,

His counter.

looks directly at me.

'What can I do for you, sir?'

The chatter continues…

What'll I say? Tell him about Jess. Justin. All I can think about is his moustache. Maybe I should just tell him his sign is on the blink?

I open my mouth to speak, but all that comes out is…

'Ahm…' followed closely by, 'Ehm…'

When, just then, and just as his shoulder radio bursts to life, he enters this exclusive other world, to which I'm not invited, and I, not for the first time, feel excluded. For some reason I recall how, so soon, after my father died my mother married 'The Dentist' and, so soon after that, got that red rose tattoo just over her right…

Ahem!

Then, of course, there was 'The Accident!?'

'The Accident!?' which resulted in so much of my childhood being played out by other children, while I recovered, first in hospital, then behind those dark, heavy curtains. And, when I did return to school, I remember how the boys taunted me while the girls just giggled, let the other boys play their kissing games.

Meantime I'm jolted back, for between several bursts of static, I cannot help but hear...

``Vehicle- Mini Cooper- Probable Taken Without Owners Consent- Negative- Unable to contact owner- Urban professional- Affirmative- Over-``

A longer burst of static is accompanied by the, hardly flattering, description of a suspect...

``On lookout for average white male- Acting in suspicious manner- Age indeterminate- Medium build- ``

Me!

``Possibly emotionally disturbed...``

After what I've been through, what do they expect?

``Negative- No distinguishing features-``

As I contemplate the relative merits of having 'No distinguishing features' I overhear...

``Last seen wearing... ``

And with that drop the jacket, kick it toward the swing doors.

Why am I so worried? All I need do is explain.

Then I hear...

``Approach with caution-``

Find I'm backing away from the counter, while he, having stopped talking, now writes. When, without looking up, he points at me, motions me forward.

And forward I go.

Almost at the counter, he indicates that I stop.

And stop I do.

I wait for him to finish. And wait. Finally he drops his pen looks up at me and...

Oh no! Bad enough he 'shot' me. He's now going to implicate me in a crime, that may or may not have occurred, and if it did occur? I didn't commit. If you follow? I'm not entirely sure I do.

'Sorry 'bout that sir. Where were we?' And then he smiles.

If you could call it that?

I try to appear composed but am let down by a body, which, amid a series of spasms and tics, has begun to mildly convulse. I'm aware I may be sending out the wrong signals of someone just described as, 'Possibly Emotionally Disturbed!'

Now uncomfortable, he starts to shuffle.

What to do? Go! I should. Shouldn't I? But I'm now overwhelmed by a need to reassure him.

And so, mid-twitch, I decide to tell him everything, however, 'Vehicle registration form!' gets blurted out instead.

He gives me a look that, very least, says, 'I don't take kindly to time wasters!' then turns, surprisingly gracefully, toward a series of shelves where he extracts the requisite document, tosses it adroitly, if not a little contemptuously, through the aperture. I take the form, fold it, put it in the inside pocket of my jacket, when, as form meets air...

Awkward!

I realize I'm not wearing it. A quizzical eyebrow gets raised as I, folded form in hand, sidle off.

Picking up the jacket I go outside, where the rain now splatters like tiny bombs; and where, colliding with an imaginary wall, I stop up suddenly…

Four

For a police woman, notebook out, is diligently examining Jess' car, recording each detail in, I'm sure, impeccable handwriting. As a gloved hand wipes rain, from sharply defined features, her police vest gets lit an intermittent orange by the flashing of the 'hazards'.

In passing I call, 'Bad day for it!' good naturedly.

Too good naturedly, given the circumstances.

She, raising a pen in acknowledgement, wonders where she heard that line before.

I shuffle on reproaching myself for relinquishing the car so easily. Soaked to the bone, more confused than ever, my head hurts as though the hangover is back. Only worse. Much, much worse. And then, of course, the chatter starts...

Justin! JUSTIN!! Justin! How could Jess do that to me? And why would she leave the car? And her phone? Why wasn't she in work? Was that Justin on the phone? Who IS Justin? Who IS JUSTIN! WHO IS JUSTIN!?

Stumbling, head in hands, I begin slapping my forehead. Pressing my hands tight against my ears I let out a, 'Who is Justin!?' find I'm now shouting my thoughts aloud, drawing looks both nervous and sympathetic

Though mainly nervous.

from anxious passers-by.

What to do? What to do? I need to know what to do.

If Jess were here she'd know exactly what to do. Why couldn't I be more like her? Decisive. Intuitive. Emotionally stable.

Or, and for tonight's star prize, is it answer (D) All the above?

I now wish I'd read that book on 'Emotional Intelligence' because, 'I don't think I can cope right now!'

Ssh! You really mustn't shout!

A finger presses against my lips…

Sorry! I don't think I can... Don't can think I... Can I think?... Don't!... I think... I think... I can't think!

As my eyes blink against the rain, my mind, like a broken engine. putters to a standstill. That's when I notice I'm making my way through a throng of pedestrians.

The way a bowling ball makes its way through tenpins.

In addition, I've not only become light headed, I may also be delirious. For just now, as I start to laugh, I seem to lose control of my legs. When, like a plane in a tail spin, I appear to be hurtling toward the ground.

All at once everything goes dark.

And stays dark until my eyes, to the sound of tapping on a window, flick open and I see not only has the weather changed, to bright sunshine, I now face a canvas canopied bookshop, where a cardboard, promotional…

Whassisname? The Old Detective. The one with hat and trench-coat.

casually leans against a neatly arranged stack of books. And from where, top lip curled, he looks down on me as if judging, or mocking me.

Harlow. Sam Harlow. Thassit!

As I read his name from a placard. When, 'Oh no!'
I definitely am delirious.

For just now, as I try to sit, I'm convinced I see him move.

'Cardboard' Harlow that is.

Raising his hat, he holds it just in front of his eyes, as though dazzled by the sun. And then, as he taps on the window again, I'm convinced I hear him say.

'Hey you!'

'Who me?'

'Yes, you Magoo! What are you a macaroon?' he stoops, pulls on the pleats of his cardboard trousers.

'Huh!?'

'You're chasing this dame and don't even know where to start.'

'B-But. How did you…?'

'You want my advice?'

I want to tell him, all things considered, 'I don't want your advice, thanks very much.' but that may have implications for my, already precarious, mental health.

I do anyway.

'I don't want your advice, thanks very much.'

'You gotta begin with the basics.' regardless.

'The b-basi...?'

'The who, what, where, when and why.' cutting across me.

'Huh?'

'You gotta ask yourself questions.'

'I d-do?'

'Was she behaving, odd?'

'No!'

'In any way, peculiar?'

'Not that I...'

'Anyone hanging around that should'na been?'

'I dunno.'

'Did she have a routine...?'

'You're not letting me think.'

'... that she broke in any way?'

'I can't thin-'

'Did she receive or make phone-calls at unusual times of the day?'

'I-I... I d-dunno.' I slur.

'Did she act in a manner that might suggest she was be playing around behind your back?' on his haunches now.

'J-Just…' I almost blurt his name.

'Just? Just what? Spit it out!'

'Justi… Just I think I'd like you to stop now.'

I think I got away with it.

'All in good time.'

'Please!'

'Did she seem distressed, agitated or upset?'

'No.'

'Irrational? Anxious? Irritable?'

'I… I…' I try to keep up, but he's going too fast.

'Did you have a fight, an argument, a quarrel?' he continues rapid-fire.

'Yes… N-no… I don't know. No!... You're confusing me.'

'Kidder you're no help. I oughta slap you in the kisser just for the heck of it.'

'Don't slap me!' I say, wanting rid of him.

Badly.

'Or, maybe you slapped her?'

'N-no! 'course not. No!' my head swims.

'Okay Kidder. I believe you.'

'Thanks.' I say, 'What you say, in mind I'll bear it. In bear I'll mind it. How much owe I do you?' I perform a charade of rooting through my pockets, find some notes, just as Harlow

Ahem.

steps through the window and, now no longer cardboard, takes my hand, licks his thumb, proceeds to count money from my palm.

It tickles. I giggle.

'Usual fee. Plus, expenses.' in that glib way of his.

Too glib for my liking. And shouldn't that be unusual fee. Ha-ha!

giving him a look, though it's he who's mad.

'Here Kidder, little something for yourself!' he says taking a note back, pressing it into my hand.

'Th-Thanks.' I say.

'I'll be seeing you.' he says.

It sounds more like 'Abyssinia?'

'When?' I say.

'In Apple Blossom Time...' he sings, makes a double-click sound with the side of his mouth when, as though about to step back through the glass, he turns, and an even more curious thing happens. For, rather than revert to his original position, he pauses, turns to face me. And I think I hear him say...

'If you want to get ahead? Get a hat!'

And that's when, hat in hand, he reaches toward me with it. And now, with his hat on my head, all I can do is splutter 'Huh?'

And it's as if the air has become charged, crackles with electricity. And then I see him back away, do a double take and, fists balled, comes right at me!?...

I try to scramble away, get as far as the bookshop window when, accompanied by a brooding rumble of thunder, that mass of charcoal cloud gets whipped into an ominous froth, the sun has gone and he, quite literally, runs right into me.

For a moment, I just stand there. When, letting out a gasp, I stumble back-wards and it begins to rain again.

And not just any rain…

Meanwhile, as I try to take in what just happened, that cloud gets lit by lightning when, 'Fzz!' an orange fork licks across the sky then, 'Uhn!' hits me in the chest.

The chest!?

and as I convulse again, violently this time, smaller forks of lightning shoot from my fingertips into the ground.

Which is when, and just as that burnt toast smell fills my nose, I find I'm on my knees and fading out…

Then in…

Then out again…

And it stays like that until someone, somewhere, finally switches out those lights.

Five

Then…

Switches them on again!

And, as I look up, it's from under the brim of Harlow's broad brimmed hat. And what I see, as my eyes readjust, is as though viewed through a sepia filter. For I seem to be in some old Hollywood film, now sit in the middle of some unnamed road and that road is lined with the classic curves of 1940's Sedans, Coupés and Convertibles while blank faced pedestrians, in shapeless dun-hued clothing, move stiffly, more formally. Including those who now shout and point…

It takes a moment, but it's 'Me' they shout and point at.

When, just then, accompanied by another 'Fzz!' of orange sparks from overhead powerlines, everything becomes 'Technicolor'. And, as I hear that noise and turn…

I wish I hadn't.

for bearing down on me is a massive streetcar, its conductors face a blur as *he* ding-dings its bell, as *it* thunders right at me!

Instinctively, I fall back and roll, just get out of its way, see I'm on the opposite track, in the path of another streetcar. Rolling again, legs inches from those scything wheels, I throw myself toward a fire hydrant, hug my arms around it. As the streetcar rumbles past I'm almost deafened by it. Then, feeling that tug on my right foot, I look down warily…

And am relieved it's only a sliver of shoe leather that lies to one side.

My relief, however, is short lived, for I'm greeted by an angry chorus of, 'Hey!',s and 'Whadda think ya doin'!?' and, 'Why doncha look where ya goin'!?' from a host of blurred faces in dark hats who throng the running boards that run alongside. A final, 'Who do ya think y'are, Joe Palooka?' gets shouted.

I don't know... Do I look like Joe Palooka?... Who's Joe Palooka?

Meanwhile, as the streetcar takes a corner, it banks sharply, and I see it has a platform to the rear.

And on that platform…

No! Couldn't be!?

a bear of a policeman

Complete with walrus moustache.

dressed in an old high-buttoned uniform and cap. And who, presumably for my benefit, beats a nightstick against the palm of his other hand. And continues to do so even as both he and the streetcar disappear under that cascade of orange sparks.

Six

I reel, let out a gasp, dust myself down

Though not necessarily in that order.

Then, getting to my feet, I reel again, for I've just seen my reflection in the bookshop window. Only more so.

How can I put this?...

It's as though I've been thrown into a cocktail shaker, mixed with a jigger of 'Essence of Harlow' and shaken. I now no longer know where I end, and 'Harlow' begins. For, apart from The Hat and Trench-coat, I'm wearing a dark wool suit with shirt and matching tie. A gunmetal tie-clip is attached third button down while a white handkerchief, pressed into a triangle, adorns my breast pocket. Taking off 'The Hat' I run a hand through my hair, am convinced its Bay Rum's vanilla/cinnamon I smell when, noticing that bulge under my left armpit...

I reach in, carefully remove a gleaming Colt .45. Looking at it a lexicon of unfamiliar words float through my head.

Words like 'Rod', 'Piece' and 'Gat'.

It's as though Harlow's in my head and I'm thinking his thoughts. Or, am I in his and he's thinking mine?

Huh!?

Holding the gun, as though the most natural thing in the world, I oddly enjoy its heft, even more oddly, find I'm familiar with it. For I remove the clip, check it, replace it. Cocking it, safety off, I slide it back into its chamois holster.

Hat on, trench-coat collar up, arms thrust deep into the pockets, I feel complete, and so heading off with a sense of purpose, knowing exactly where to go and what to do, without looking, I step into the road, get met by a belligerent chorus of shouts, car-horns, and slapped door panels. Undaunted I proceed to weave my way across…

Until, that is, I get to the other side, find not only is my way blocked, it's blocked by another policeman in a similar, high-buttoned, uniform.

This one, however, is young, has a familiarly grim face. As I try to pass his right-hand presses against my chest. When, just then his left shoots out, and a solitary raindrop spatters into the palm of his black, leather glove.

'Bad day for it!' he says. Donning Aviator sunglasses he tips his cap, turns on a jack-booted heel and is gone.

I reassure myself…

It's only a dream.

when, and accompanied by a most decisive…

'Aw shaddup!' the all new 'I, Me Harlow' is born. And he/I, interjects…

'Why did'n'ya just shoot him?'

Huh!?

'My world, my rules.'

What is going on?

'Oh, you'll find out Kidder. Meantime turnaround.'

And, as I turn,

Or is that now we?

I find I'm at the foot of a, high stepped, brownstone building, facing a sign with gilt, gothic lettering.

What the…!?

As a bell rings a voice echoes, a girlish, singsong voice, for the sign reads, Harbinger and Associates. I take a moment then, two at a time, run up the steps. I come to a door with an intercom to one side. Normally I'd press, wait for a reply.

But not today.

For just now, without buzzing, I've made my way through and into a dusty reception area where I'm greeted by a blue-eyed, peroxide 'Bombshell'.

I know, but it's not like I can help it.

She's too busy applying scarlet lipstick to those bee-stung lips of hers to even notice me. So, I go over, drop my hat in front of her, perch, one leg swinging, on her desk. She swivels her chair, moves a silver, pearl handled, mirror to one side, and bats me,

Out of the ballpark!

with those lashes of hers.

As Nat 'King' Cole croons 'Nature Boy', through the crackle of a table-top radio, from somewhere I produce a gold cigarette case. Removing one I tap it, toss it and

Bear with me.

catch it in the corner of my mouth. Opening a battered Zippo, I roll it across my thigh. It ignites. I light up, take a drag, am in the process of blowing a second smoke ring through its larger cousin,

I think I like this, 'I, Me Harlow'.

when she, cupping my hand in hers, turns the cigarette toward her. As she sucks down on the filter tip she pulls herself up, stretches across the desk. Breathing her smoke into my mouth, for a tantalizing moment her lips brush mine then, her eyes never leaving me, she sidles back into her chair.

'Hey Dollface! Where ya been all my life?' I say, blowing out her smoke.

And in a voice, mine, yet not mine.

'Your life ain't over yet!' when, with a squeak of unoiled castors, she pushes her chair back, gives me the full picture; black stockings and pencil skirt worn just below tight, white cashmere. I'm transfixed. She knows it. Shaking a tiny bottle, without looking, she starts to flick red varnish over long, almond nails. I could watch her all day. Until that voice reminds me...

'Hey Kidder! There's work to be done.'

And then the phone rings. She's too busy blowing on her nails so I snatch it from its cradle. Toying with her, make as though to answer it.

No, I definitely like this, 'I, Me Harlow'.

Arching me with an eyebrow, the 'Me' that's in here still, hands it back.

'Hello Harbinger and Associates. How may I help you?' her voice changes, all at once it's girlish, singsong.

That bell again.

Cupping the receiver in both hands, she swivels away. I lean slightly in, just enough to make out a muffled, male voice,

There's something about his voice that I...

I lean in closer. In the background I hear music, from another time, another place, I barely make it out, but it's...

That 'Gnossienne'.

She hangs up, swivels back to face me...

'Now.' her voice least an octave lower, her tone exclusive, suggestive.

'Hm-hmm!' I clear my throat.

'How may I help you?'

I'm flummoxed, until that is, I find I'm reaching inside my jacket, pulling out a black and white head-shot of Jess.

No. I don't know how it got there either.

I toss it on the desk.

'I'm cherchezing the femme.' I say, or rather, I, Me Harlow, says through me.

'Oh. Is she, fatale?'

'You tell me.'

'How should I know?'

'This Harbinger and Associates?'

'Says so on the door.'

'She's works here.'

'Can't say that I…' shifting in her chair.

'Goes by the name of Grimason. Jess Grimason.'

She clicks on an Angle-poise lamp, picks up the photo. At the same time, she stretches out a leg, one that seems to take forever to unfurl. I glance down, notice she balances a black stiletto on her toes. She catches me, for she looks down at her shoe then, very slowly, back up at me. I loosen my tie as suddenly it's gotten hot in here.

'Well?' I, Me Harlow says, 'Whadda ya think and whadda ya know?'

'You only want my thoughts?' her fingers play with a looped gold earring.

'Uh-huh.' I nod, as she shimmies out of her chair.

'You sure?' flattening the creases of her skirt, hands on hips, with all the skill of a tightrope walker, she sashays toward me, purrs. 'Will you give me a penny for them?'

'I'm just trying to find Jess.' I gulp.

'My thoughts. We were talking about my thoughts.'

'What? Oh, were we?'

Her fingers reaching up, she straightens my lapels.

'Hm-hmm!'

'Something wrong with your throat?'

I use the handkerchief to wipe a trail of drool from my chin when,

Thankfully.

I, Me Harlow takes over again.

'Look Dollface. You're trouble. The sort of sweet trouble, a man doesn't need yet somehow does. I'll give you a dollar each for a hundred of them. Do you have that many thoughts?'

'Tut-tut-tut.' her tone scolding.

I reach into my pocket pull out a wad. It's rolled tight, held by a rubber band, contains $100 dollars.

Don't ask.

'What, ehm, had you in mind?'

'We could start with who that was on the phone then we could take a walk round the block and you could tell me all you know 'bout a character, name of Justin.'

She makes a grab for the greenbacks when...

'Ah-ah.' I, Me Harlow grabs her wrist.

'That hurt,' she pouts, pulling away, 'That how you get off Mister? Getting rough with poor, vulnerable girls?'

'Sister you cut your way out of the womb, weaned yourself on barbed wire and razor blades.'

She throws her head back, laughs, 'What if I say I don't know no Justin?'

'No show. No dough.'

'Hmm. Let me see now…' she strokes her chin, 'give me the dough I tell ya all I know.'

'Ah-ah. Tell me what you know, then I give you the dough.' I, Me Harlow produces another wad, 'Plus a donation to a charity of your choice.'

'Mother Maria's Orphanage?'

'Funny, I thought it'd be 'The Home for Poor, Vulnerable Girls.'

'It is now. Mister...?'

'No names, no pack drill.'

And no, I don't know what it means.

'Either way you got a deal. Shake?'

As she extends her hand and I take it, I'm transfixed by her nails, for they have the texture and sheen of polished blood, in fact I'm so taken by them I don't immediately notice, in her other hand she holds a silver, pearl handled, revolver.

It matches her mirror.

'Uh-oh!'

Training the gun, she relieves I, Me Harlow of the wads, puts them in her purse.

'That what poor, vulnerable girls get for Christmas?'

'Only the good ones.'

For a moment, all is still. When...

No don't!

I, Me Harlow reaches for the .45... Crack! her muzzle flashes and 'Unh!' the bullet rips into my chest.

The chest!?

As I hit the floor, Nat's still singing, ``A little shy and sad of eye, but very wise was he...``

Which could easily be my epitaph,

'cept, of course, for the 'wise' bit.

Dollface, meanwhile, kneels over me, whispers in my ear, 'By the way, Justin sends his love!'

I'm about to say, 'No! Not Justin.' when she straddles me, pulls me up by the lapels, plants a deep, lush smacker square on my lips. Despite everything a voice inside my head tells me...

What a way to go!

And then, it's as though somebody, somewhere...

Switches out those lights again!

Seven

Then switches them on again…

And I seem to be back outside the bookshop, under its rain-drummed canopy. Strained faces tower over me, some with apparent concern. I try to speak but it's as though my tongue has withered, died at the back of my throat.

I gather someone calls, 'Don't move him!'

While someone else calls, 'Somebody call an ambulance!'

But as they shout, each over the other, what I hear is a confusion of words. 'Somebody... Don't... call an... move... ambulance... him!'

Followed by a less concerned, 'Probably a junkie!'

And then…

'Yeah, or a psycho!'

My faith in humanity is restored as someone points at me, laughs, 'Look, he's foaming at the mouth. Never saw one of them do that before.'

And with that,

Most gratefully.

I fall away again.

Eight

Only to be roused by extreme discomfort for, apart from the bullet, I feel nauseous. Caused by the undulations of whatever it is carries me. And then, there's the rank smell of rotting fish and that other smell, a separate, stale animal aroma.

It doesn't take long to discover the reason for the undulations is because I'm being transported on the, not inconsiderable shoulder, of something called 'Ox';

The source, seemingly, of the aroma.

I know he's called Ox for I hear Dollface call out. 'Don't worry if you let him drop Ox!'

As he turns his head, grunts in return, I get a glimpse of possibly the most inhuman face I've ever seen. A crazy paving of patchwork features, the result either of an aberration of nature, or the work of an incompetent surgeon. A surgeon who, not only botched his job, but proceeded to rectify the damage with a broken brick.

From behind, through a dense yellow fog, Dollface's patent leather stilettos click and clack hammer click-clicks on empty chambers. It's only when Ox, seemingly impervious to the bullets, places his massive 'mitt' around her soft white, throat that her laughter stops.

Ox, the light leaving his eyes, and in an act, that from a distance, could be mistaken for tenderness, bear-hugs her to him. Then, almost casually, stepping off the pier, he

Needless-to-say.

takes Dollface with him.

And that's all until, with a thunderous slosh, I see them sink. Meanwhile, caught in their wake, as though by some invisible hand, I get pulled deeper and deeper. Which is when, starting to panic, I pull off the trench-coat, kick out. Snorting seawater, I somehow scrabble to the surface, where…

But how?

the three nuns from the funeral car, now occupy Dollface's space. And I'm compelled by them as they take turns to step forward, toss a single red rose into the dark, surging water, as though to mark the spot I went in.

'I'm okay. I'm over here!' I call but they don't hear, and with the fog thicker than ever, don't see me either. Instead they begin a lament so poignant the brief snatch I hear almost reduces me to tears.

'I'm stretched on your grave and will lie there forever…'

I don't wish to split hairs, but…

Meanwhile, I find I'm getting pulled by that invisible hand again. It's only as I go under, can no longer breathe that I realize…

This time the hand seems real.

Nine

For Ox's 'mitt' is locked tight on to my ankle and the light very much back in his eyes, which, as he pulls me under, are blood red and all that's visible.

'Have I got this right Kidder? You're just gonna drown with him!'

What else can I do?

'Kick him with all ya got.'

I can't do that.

But I do, do that, and do kick him with, all I got. Which, even Ox would admit, isn't much. Then suddenly, he begins to jerk. Only this time, as he releases my foot, there's a look of shock on his face. I feel sorry for Ox, falling away like that, fingers splayed as though still trying to hold onto me. And I still feel sorry for him as that pounding beats in my temples and my lungs seem fit to burst. And, as I can no longer make it to the surface, I start to jerk too. Finally, as everything becomes deathly still, like a sodden ragdoll, I just hang there, listless.

Until that is, something tugs at the hole in my chest. I'm too numb to feel any more pain, but I do notice a purple ooze has begun to trail out and away from me. Looking up, I see a long wooden pike, hear it swish through the water. Then, as its pointed metal barb enters my chest, I find I'm being hooked like a fish. And, as I become animated again, the pain is back. Only worse. Much, much worse.

So much worse that I… that I… that I…

And, as everything turns black, a deep, impenetrable, black, my eyes inexorably screw closed.

Ten

And they stay that way for quite some time, least 'til they flick open and

Huh!?

I become dazzled by those lights.

And that's when

To the sound of cheers and discordant notes from a Wurlitzer organ.

I see that silhouette dance down that flight of neon stairs. And, then it occurs to me…

I'm in a studio, on some sort of 'Game Show'…

'Come on in folks it's great to see ya, I mean that, I really do.'

Delivered, I'm sure, with a knowing wink; for I still can't make out his face.

'And on offer on tonight's, Question of a Lifetime,' pointing at me, 'The never to be repeated opportunity of… Now wait for it.'

Accompanied by a drum roll and more cheers.

'That's right, 'Uh-uh! Uh-uh! Staying alive!' To the sound of clashing cymbals. 'And all you have to do is answer one question. Course should you be unable to answer that question... Well you'll have to pay the forfeit.'

Met by boos from the audience. The vacant, grinning audience that couldn't look more one-dimensional were they photographic cut-outs.
Which, as it happens, they are.

'Yes, that's right... With your life!' emphasized by a 'Wah-wah!' from the organ.

As he steps to one side, a red velvet curtain falls away to reveal a polished wooden crossbow, fixed to the ground, aimed squarely at me. Which is when, as I try to move, I realize I'm manacled hand and foot to a large neon Spinning Wheel.
Believe me, I feel the same...!?

And then, as a hush descends, he's back, 'Now, with tonight's question and a big hand on her entrance. Miaow! The One! The Only! The Hostess with The Most-est!'

To the sound of wolf whistles and lewd cheers, a spotlight turns on a series of dangerous curves held tight together by diamante and sequins,
I know, I know.

who moves with a distinctive click-clack while carrying a tasselled cushion. And on that cushion, a gold envelope that she presents to The Host, who proceeds to pat her on her

Ahem.

posterior. She, for her part, seems to enjoy it and pretends to claw at him like a cat.

There's something so wrong, and in so many ways, about all of this.

Then, and in that way of hers, she's sashaying toward me.

'I thought you were dea-' I say as she turns, puts a finger to my lips, assumes a pose behind me at The Wheel.

Suddenly the lights dim, and an up-light turns on him, giving him grotesque, distorted, features.

'And now, the moment we've all been waiting for, for it's...' Yet another drum roll. 'The Question of a Lifetime!'

To the sound of cheers and stomping, he opens the envelope, removes a card.

'Audience are you ready?' Face still distorted,

he turns to face them, then back to me. 'And you sir? Are you ready?'

'No! I'm no-' Dollface clamps my jaw, forces my head into a nod.

'Great! We're all ready.' smacking his lips, 'Now if you please Billy to your post.'

I watch helplessly as a small, thin man with an angular face, sunken eyes and large teeth steps into the light, acknowledges the

Ahem.

crowd, takes up position behind the crossbow.

There's something about him and those teeth that I recog-?

'Ssh!' Our Host takes the card, whispers 'Ssh!' again. And you could hear a pin drop.

As if to illustrate my point he produces a pin, does precisely that.

Then, looking toward Dollface, 'If you will?'

She, in turn, reaches up, spins 'The Wheel'. And as it spins; faster and faster still, I close my eyes until, accompanied by another clash of cymbals, all at once. It stops.

As I open my eyes I'm so disoriented and dazzled by a kaleidoscope of light everything seems psychedelic. So much so I can't make anything (or anyone) out but I do hear that chant...

'The question! The question! Ask the question!'

And there's palpable tension as he commands, 'Ssh!' again. And another hush descends just as a blinding spotlight turns on me. And I'm even more dazzled as he, still up-lit, looks right at me...

'Where is she?'

'Wha...? I-I dunno what you mean.'

I don't like this.

'What have you done with her?'

'Jess? My Jess?'

'Billy the bolt!'

My head begins to clear, in time to see Billy load a glinting bolt into the crossbow's mechanism.

What is it about him and those teeth?

'Last chance!'

And then, as I shake my head, he winks at Billy...

Billy. 'Billy Bones'! How could I forget.

Then... Whoosh! that bolt

Needless-to-say.

tears into my chest, the pain is back, my eyes screw closed and stay like that...

Eleven

Until, with a gasp, they flick open again and that's when I see him.

Him and his walrus moustache and his uniform cap and his yellow oilskins dripping rainwater.

And, as he hauls me over the gunwale of an old Police boat, removes the pike from my chest, drops me onto its heaving deck, I get a strange feeling,

Déjà vu all over again!

for, as I'm now back in 'Harlow's World', I need to tell him 'Very least, one of us shouldn't be here.' but before I can I find I'm getting pulled up by the lapels.

'Where is she?' he demands.

I also need to tell him I, Me Harlow is on the job and we've a definite lead. Justin. Not only is he behind all this, he thinks that he and Jess are... Anyway, he's using Harbinger and Associates as some sort of front and we should be working on this together. As for Dollface...

Her, you should approach with extreme caution!

But I'm now in so much pain and so delirious I find I'm singing.

Kind of.

'Row, row, row your boa…' then, 'Has boat this… taken been… owner's consent… without?'

'What!?'

He's not happy.

'Row, row, row your boat gently down the stream…'

He lets go my lapels, wraps my tie around his wrist.

'Row, row, row your boat…'

'Where is she?' as he pulls tighter a wind begins to pick up.

'Gently down the stream...' I've forgotten the next line.

'What have you done with her?' tighter still.

'Aha!... Merrily, merrily, merrily, merrily...'

'Where is she!?' the wind, now a low moan, tugs at his oilskins.

'… life is but a dream!'

'You killed her! Didn't you?'

Transfixed, I shake my head, look at him blankly. I'm about to tell him 'No! You've made some dreadful mistake.' but instead I spew all over his police badge, across his oilskins and down into his galoshes. I had hoped he might have been repulsed, push me away. If anything, he pulls me closer, my tie even tighter.

Then, as that wind begins to stiffen and whip around the deck. With an, 'Up and at 'em, Kidder!'
Thankfully
I, Me Harlow takes over. And I find I'm reaching inside my jacket for the .45 and then, of course, the chattering starts.
I can't. Couldn't just shoot someone. Not in cold bloo-?
'Kidder, as I said, my world, my rules. Kill or get killed!'
Which
As if I hadn't enough on my plate.
is when the deck begins to rise and my tie, pulled so tight I begin to choke. And yet my fingers, so close to the gun.
Nearly there...

'This what you're looking for?' he grabs my arm, releases my tie.

As I nod, he levels the .45...

'No. Please, don't!'

Bang!...

Just as he squeezes the trigger, a huge wave surges over the deck, the boat yaws we both lose footing and the bullet whistles over my head. As I scramble to my feet he's already on his. Then, as that second wave hits, the boat lists, we both topple backwards...

Rolling across the deck, 'Unh!' I collide with the capstan, only avoid getting swept overboard by grabbing onto it. Buffeted by wind, pounded by waves, I cling on. Until, that is, that even bigger wave crashes over and I'm sent careering across the deck, slammed against the port gunwale. I'm only spared being swept over by the boat, suddenly, regaining a more even keel.

More than can be said for me.

Meanwhile, as the wind begins to calm, and the boat continues to right itself, my only consolation, he's nowhere to be seen. And then, as I get to my feet, it occurs to me…

Someone must be piloting the boat.

And, as I turn to face the wheel-house, I see Young Grim Face. And he sees me too, for he tips his cap, nods at me. It's only as I nod back, that hand grabs my shoulder…

It wasn't me he was nodding to at all. And he still has the .45.

Him and his walrus moustache and his yellow oilskins…

Then, pulling down on the trigger, he smiles

If you could call it that?

as… Bang! He shoots me in the chest.

Twelve

And 'Unh!' as I go over the side I'm falling away again, deeper than before. Only this time a curious thing happens. For the water, rather than engulf me, seems to enfold me. And it's like I'm in some sort of a womb. As there's no I, Me Harlow to contradict, I curl up, succumb quite contentedly.

And I'm so content there, in my watery cocoon, I go as far as resisting whoever it is, that pulls on my arm...

Thirteen

'Leave me alone!' I splutter, seemingly no longer underwater, but now back in front of the bookshop and under its rain-drummed canopy. I blink, then blink again, but there's no mistake. For, standing there, right in front of me, still in her oyster blouse is Jess!?

'Get up!' she says.

'I can't.' I reply

'Why not?'

'My chest hurts. I've been shot'

'You haven't been shot!'

'I have!' I look down then up again. I'm perplexed, for the bullet-hole is gone.

'Why does my chest hurt so?'

'I broke your heart.'

'Oh!'

'Sorry.'

She tries to console me by squeezing my arm, but I'm not in a forgiving mood and pull it away.

'Who's Justin?' I say.

Her expression changes. It's as though she looks at me but sees someone else. She becomes fearful, starts to back away. I grab her wrist. The strength of my grip surprises me. She tries hard to pull away, but I won't let go. Not even as I tell her, 'I'm sorry Jess. I didn't mean to I…'

Meanwhile, though she tries to hide it behind her back, I can tell she has something in her other hand. 'What's in your hand?' I ask.

By way of reply, she kneels on top of me, forces whatever it is into my mouth, pulls away.

'What are you doin-?' I try to ask, but as my throat is now full of sand, I cough. And I cough again as I try to reach out to her, but she just backs further, and further, into the rain. Until finally, she's gone. And then, not long after, still coughing sand, I'm gone too.

Fourteen

And I'm still coughing sand as I find I'm no longer in front of the bookshop but am instead lying face-down…

On some beach!?

A beach where a shimmering sun gives everything a silvery veneer and where I'd be burnt to a crisp were it not for the fronds of the palm tree that shade me. As I lie there, wondering when all this is going to end

Anytime now would be good.

I look down, as I've started to feel a nipping and tugging on my left hand.

And that's when I see my hand has dipped into a rock-pool where a family of razor clawed crabs now feast on it. On my feet, I manage to shake them off, pulling out my handkerchief, I wrap the linen around the remnants of my fingers, and note how badly they hurt. Though not as much as the rest of me. I peep gingerly inside my shirt, notice the bullet-hole has returned, now oozes a purple matter. I make a mental note to Jess.

Told you so.

Meanwhile, after managing to button my jacket, a breeze picks up, blows flurries of sand over a series of grassy dunes. And, as the breeze stiffens, the flurries become mini tornadoes that whip across the beach, as I raise my hands to shield my face they merge to form a single vortex. And that's when it occurs to me…

I'm right in its eye!

Suddenly it's dark and silent, apart from that shrill whistling that makes my eardrums feel they're about to pop. And just as I begin to suffocate, I stumble forward, the sand falls away, and I'm able to breathe again. And yet I still hear whistling. Only now I recognize it…

Fifteen

'The Gnossienne'...

And, as I rise, I see it's comes from a gaunt man

With a jaded demeanour.

who's dressed in a butler's uniform; consisting of wing collar, bowler hat, bow tie. And I'm compelled by him, as he almost glides across the sand while carrying a silver salver. And on it, a full cocktail glass; complete with olive on a stick. Oh, and a metal drum the size of a biscuit tin!?

When he reaches the shoreline he removes the glass, hands it to the fat, bald, man, who has just waddled naked from the sea. And who, just now, has downed his drink in one. The butler, producing a previously unseen, green paisley, dressing gown helps the fat man into it.

And that's when I shudder...

For, even from this distance, I see the fat man's head is scarred, his eyebrows non-existent. Then, as he unscrews the lid from the drum, he applies fine, white, powder to his pate and face.

The powder spirals upward, in tiny plumes, as it covers his scars. Which is when, my mouth still full of sand, I splutter the name, 'Justin.'

And as he turns, looks right at me, not only does my heart begins to gallop, but that purple matter oozes through my jacket, trickles into the rock-pool, where the crabs have now retreated. And then, as I'm in that tailspin again, I slump, face forward, into the sand. And I stay like that until the hackles at the back of my neck have been raised. It didn't require his blowing on them to do so.

But he did anyway.

Sixteen

And, as I turn, he stands over me blocking out the sun.

'W-Where's Jess?' I stutter.

'Like one that on a lonely road, Doth walk in fear and dread…' he rasps, his lips brushing my ear. 'And having once turned around walks on. And turns no more his head…'

When, just then, 'Are you just gonna lie there, Kidder?' I, Me Harlow

At last!

makes his return.

'Because he knows some frightful fiend doth close behind him tread...' leaning back, arms akimbo, he starts to laugh.

Meanwhile, and with an, 'Up and at 'im Kidder.' I'm on my feet charging Justin. I'm surprised how only the smallest push makes him lose balance, fall over. And as I scramble away, I don't get far. For, not only my path is blocked by the butler

And his jaded demeanour…

he, having put aside his tray, now points a Luger pistol at me.

However, it only takes a 'Now listen up Kidder!' to realize, he hasn't bargained on the return of I, Me Harlow or, the sand just thrown into his face. He also should've been more careful where he left his salver. For that's what we use to hit him.

Meanwhile, as I half run/half stumble across the beach, I find I'm being reproached by an indignant I, Me Harlow…

'Why didn'ya take the gun?'

I'm remonstrating with an,

Easy for you to say...

when the first bullet zips past my cheek, pockmarks the dune ahead. I glance back, see Justin now has the Luger. Then, as I stumble again, the second bullet whizzes over my head. As I clamber upward, the third and fourth punch round my feet. The fifth bullet I hear, but don't see, for I've already made my way over the dune and off the beach.

Seventeen

On my knees,

In every sense.

I'm at a dusty roadside where overhead telegraph wires cut an 'S' through a range of dried out hills and where a scaly lizard scuttles from behind a hollow log, looks at me with a wary, hooded eye.

'Don' sp'ose you know where I could get a car?' I pant.

He sticks out a thin, forked tongue.

'I only asked!' I reply, affronted.

He then turns his head as if to point across the road.

Maybe I'm reading too much into this?

'My apologies.' I say, as I turn and face a huge hoarding where a giant, neon 'Grease Monkey' wields an oversize spanner, while in his other hand, a large oilcan squirts out the legend…

'OTTO's AUTO's! STICK DRIVE OR OTTO-MATIC? WE HAVE THE OTTO-MOBILE FOR YOU! AND WE DELIVER… JUSTIN TIME!'

As I contemplate should there be a space between 'JUST' and 'IN'. Coming over that rise I almost don't hear the thrum of that finely tuned engine. Stepping into the road, arms in frantic semaphore, I try to flag it down. And then as it shows no sign of stopping and I'm unable to get out of its path…

That's when it hits me!

Literally.

Eighteen

'Oof!' as I get catapulted high above the sweeping curves of an open top Packard Convertible,

It says on the grille.

'Aha!' I have an epiphany. A moment of absolute clarity, where everything that has happened makes perfect sense and falls neatly into place. Only to promptly get forgotten as 'Unh!' I hit the ground.

It takes several moments to appreciate I'm not road kill. I try to roll onto my back; can't quite make it. When... Vroom! The Packard reverses and, as I can't get out of its way, I close my eyes, tense for impact.

Exhaust heat on my cheek, just short of my head... It stops.

As the passenger door swings wide, I use it to get to my feet. That's when I see her!?

Her and that familiar pointy chin that juts just below those crimson lips. And that dress with its familiar floral print and those novelty pink slippers...

'Sorry. I didn't see you I…'

I want to say, 'How could you not see me?' but the words just won't come.

'Please… please get in.'

Not that I'm standing up for her but she, anxiously looking over her shoulder, does appears quite distracted. As she opens the door wider and I fall in, she says something quite odd. Something that sounds like…

'There, there. Not to worry, Mother's here.'

'You're not… Not my mother!' I cough, as she dons a pair of white sunglasses, fastens them in place with a headscarf, giving another glance over her shoulder, pulls suddenly away.

Yielding to that soft, creamy upholstery my eyelids begin to close, and I drift off. Which was unfortunate, for had they not, I may have noticed that old Rolls Royce Phantom in the wing mirror, and may also have noticed that The Butler, having exchanged his uniform for one of a chauffeur's, gives scant regard to his scarred passenger, sitting impassively to the rear. Dressed, as he still is, in his green paisley.

Nineteen

And, when my eyelids open, I find not only have we left the desert landscape behind, we're now on a steep ascent. Which is when she pats me on the cheek, insists…

'Sleep my baby. Sleep'

'Won't sleep… Not your baby' I tell her, sitting up.

She then begins to hum 'Brahms Lullaby' as I, initially impervious, begin to succumb, and that's when we take that bend too fast the door swings wide again, only this time… I fall out.

Twenty

My face inches from the road, I see we are dangerously close to the edge of a precipitous cliff. I gasp as she grabs my jacket, pulls me back in.

I ask her to stop, or at least slow down. 'Stop. Or, at least slow down!' I say.

And that's when I notice the determination on her face as she floors the gas, pulls down on the big, white wheel and tears around another bend still, every so often, glancing over her shoulder.

'W-Where are we going!?' I stutter as the 'speedo' needle hovers around the dangerous end of the dial.

'Home,' she says, 'I've come to take you home!' in a tone I find oddly comforting.

And, as the end of her scarf falls away, I see that red rose tattoo just over her right...

And then, for some strange reason I blurt, 'I want to go home. Please Mother take me home.'

And it's like I'm a child again as she smiles, pats me reassuringly on the cheek.

And that's when we get the first 'Bump!'…

Twenty-one

I say 'Bump', to be fair it was little more than a gentle shunt…

The second 'Bump!' however, was much less gentle and, given the power of 'The Rolls', adequate to whip me against the dash, render me unconscious, and propel the Packard's white-wall tires out, over the edge of the cliff…

Where it now begins to seesaw!…

And where, as I come to, any sudden movement makes it, 'Whoah!' dip suddenly. And then, stomach heaving, I notice she's gone. I glance back, over the soft top where floral dress flapping, I see not only her but who's with her. Justin.

And he sees me too for, as he gives the slightest nod, 'The Rolls' looms into view, flicks on its headlights, powers right at me.

Twenty-two

I clamber into the driver's seat, my hands, feet dance across the various, levers and pedals. As I struggle to make sense of them all, I hit the radio and ``Get Happy``

If only!

burst's out.

I try the ignition. The engine grinds. I try it again. 'Whoah!' I'm staring into a watery abyss, for, as the ledge below partly gives way, the Packard inches further over the edge. Meanwhile, as the engine grinds again, over my shoulder, I see the impassive features of 'The Butler' as he closes in on me. And I, not knowing what else to do, start to panic...

Until, that is, with a 'C'mon Kidder!' that voice fights its way into my head and I'm nodding as the engine roars to life. And, as I, Me Harlow finds reverse, the Packard growls up the incline, slews back onto the road just as 'The Rolls', like some ghost car, glides past, shoots off the cliff. I even see 'The Butler' glance sideways

His demeanour more jaded than ever

as the 'Rolls' flies a moment, dips suddenly, and with a 'Toot, Toot, Tootsie Goodbye!' from the radio, is gone.

I don't look down, but I do see a vivid, orange fireball, hear a low, percussive rumble, as both car and driver get dashed against the rocks below. Turning my head, I notice the unlikely pair, in their respective floral print and green paisley, are now in the middle of the road.

I'm particularly taken by her, for she seems in genuine distress, looking first to him, then to me, as though she cannot decide between us. Justin then grabs her wrist. She glares at him. He grabs her other wrist. She shakes her head. For a moment it's like they're actors in some silent film until, 'Eek!' she screams and pulls away. Only this time she runs toward the cliff-edge. Then giving me that look

The one that's strangely forlorn.

with a final flap-flap of her dress, she closes her eyes and jumps.

'No! Please don't!' I shout, but it's already too late.

For a moment, time stands still. Justin looks stunned as though confused what next to do. I, for my part, feel surprisingly sad, find I'm wiping away tears.

And then, as that bullet shatters my tail light, I see that Justin, lacking my sentimentality, has begun to shoot. Instinctively I disengage the handbrake, pull urgently away, oblivious of the brake fluid trail left behind me.

Twenty-three

And so, on a steep ascent, Justin now far behind, I try to piece everything together, but am overcome by sadness

As my sodden cuff testifies.

for I keep remembering that look she gave me, just before she...

Meanwhile, as I ease into another bend, I find, at least, I'm becoming versed in the ways of the Packard. When, and just as 'Stormy Weather' plays on the radio, that bank of charcoal cloud rolls in again and it begins to rain.

And not just any rain...

For, as it sluices across the wind-shield, the wiper blade is ineffective against it. I look down, see a pool has formed under my feet. Reaching back, to pull up the soft top, I pump the brake and find, rather than slow, the Packard speeds up disproportionately. And then, through the driving rain…

I think I see a truck!?

Twenty-four

A truck whose headlights shoot fangs of light as, amid a spray of sparks, we collide side on. It, canopy flapping, almost topples over, then, bouncing on its suspension, rights itself.

Meanwhile all I can do is pull on the handbrake as, rear wheels locked, the Packard slides from under me, aquaplanes out over the edge. When, as I floor the gas, pull down hard on the wheel, to the sound of shale splashing and that fading, dissonant honk, I find

Thankfully.

I'm back on the road.

The road which, before I can take any solace, has, quite unexpectedly, dropped away, dipping suddenly to become a spectacular descent. With the rain, heavier than ever, and the car travelling at breakneck momentum, I don't see that 'Road Ahead Closed!' sign until it's almost too late...

It's only as the Packard, as though with a mind of its own, swerves down that smaller unmarked road, do I see the coastal landscape has given way to a muddy, more rural one. While up ahead, lit by two hurricane lamps, a wooden barricade looms out of the dark. And, as I slam headlong into it, I nearly don't notice that the barricade has a sign. Or, that the sign reads...

'Stop Police!'

Twenty-five

And then, even though dazed, my vision blurred, at the side of the road I see it…

The old black and white police car, engine ticking over, as its former occupants, police badges glinting, stride toward me. Young Grim Face, still wearing those sunglasses, twirls a nightstick from a cord around his wrist, announces 'Bad day for it.' passes toward the rear. His companion,

Him and his walrus moustache and his uniform cap and his yellow oilskins dripping rainwater.

now standing over me, asks…

'How we doing there?'

'F-fine.' I say, blinking away rain.

'I wasn't talking to you.' he replies.

'Left tail light out.'

'The right?'

I turn my head in time to see him swing his nightstick. When, and to the accompaniment of breaking glass, 'It's out too.'

'You know, round here, to lose one tail light is unfortunate but to lose two, well…'

'That's downright criminal.' his partner joining him.

'What should we do with him?'

'I don't rightly know.'

I'm like a spectator at a tennis match looking first to one. Then, the other.

'Maybe were he to cooperate, tell us what he did with the girl?'

'Given past experience, he's not the cooperating type.' patting his moustache.

'Maybe I should ask?'

'Maybe you should.'

'Are you going to cooperate?' Young Grim Face removing his sunglasses, eyeballing me.

'Yes, 'c-course I will.' I say.

'He says he will not, under any circumstances, cooperate?'

'What!... No!... I didn't!... I...' wondering where I, Me Harlow has gone, I find I'm wishing, desperately, for his return.

And anytime now would be good!

'What should we do with him?'

'Please! If you'd only listen…' I say.

Young Grim Face grabs my jaw, forces my mouth open, looks inside, 'What do you think?'

Still patting his moustache, his bearlike colleague joins him, 'Oh, dear me,' he shakes his head, 'I think we need to make an appointment with…'

'You don't mean…?'

'I'm afraid I do...'

In unison they turn and look at me, 'The Dentist!''

And I say, 'No! Please no! Not, 'The Dentist!''

All of a sudden, 'Young Grim Face' points, as though seeing something in the distance. And, as my eyes follow his, I'm unaware he raises his nightstick then… Thwack! brings it down on my head.

For a moment all is silent, a trickle of warm blood runs the length of my nose as a fog descends, I still make out their shapes but it's like they occupy a space just outside my normal vision. And that's when, as I seem to fall, I see Young Grim Face's outline and he stands at an impossibly acute angle to me. Next thing I know he's sitting me upright in the passenger seat while he eases into the driver's seat.

'Get some rest. You'll need it.' he says, sitting me upright again.

'I want to go home. Please Mother take me home.' I tell him.

And then I seem to fall again, only this time he just lets me fall. And so fall I do. Fall and spin. Spin and fall.

Deeper and deeper…

And deeper into my 'self'.

And as I fall I feel like I'm like James Stewart in that film. The one where he falls. And then I'm dizzy, so very dizzy, it's as though I've got…

What was that film called again?

Twenty-six.

And when I finally stop falling...

I'm back, back in that childhood place, where even bad times have their own peculiar magic, and I'm bouncing my red ball so hard and so fast, both ball and hand have become a blur. And then, looking up, I see him...

Him and his angular face and dark sunken eyes and those teeth of his.

'Perks of the profession,' he'd say then clack them together by way of demonstration. To me he is the shark from 'Jaws' in human form.

'Billy Bones' that is…

'Billy Bones' is my name for 'The Dentist', my mother's new husband. I call him this, not just because he's so skinny, but also because I see him as a destructive interloper. Not unlike him in 'Treasure Island' (my then 'best' book). And he has set up practice in that small dark room at the front our house. The one with the Venetian Blinds. Oh, and he made my mother get that terrible tattoo.

And now, along with those skinny fingers of his, he has taken my ball, hidden it behind his bony back and dares me, as he backs away into the garden, come get it. I'm not sure if he plays or toys with me but I follow him anyway, making the occasional half-hearted grab for the ball, but he's too quick.

Then he throws the ball to the edge of the garden, where it bounces off our glasshouse, lodges high in the spiny willow tree. As I go to retrieve it, he grabs me, tickles me. Those long, skinny, fingers hurt more than they tickle. As I roll in the grass, pretending to laugh, he takes my ankles, starts to spin me around and around, faster and faster still. Until finally I've left the ground.

In fairness, I find it initially exciting. Until, that is, I get dizzy, ask him to stop.

'Stop!' I say.

But he ignores me, keeps on spinning me.

I tell him, 'I'm going to be sick!'

He continues regardless.

As I look into his face, see his smile. I shudder. For I see his face has darkened and his 'smile' is really a sneer. And then, he lets go...

As I sail through the air... Whoosh! Everything, for that moment, is as exhilarating as childhood can be. Everything, that is, bar the part where I collide with the glasshouse. Now, what was that old saying?

Oh yes...

People with glasshouses shouldn't throw kids!

My mother comes running, lifts me into her arms, holds me tight. I know I'm bleeding because of the little sprays that stain her floral print dress and from the droplet that has landed on her rose tattoo, almost indistinguishable against those crimson lips of hers. I notice too she wears those novelty pink slippers (the ones I bought her for Christmas).

'Billy Bones' meanwhile, stands over us and just in front of the willow. Looking up at him, I'm unsure where the tree ends, and he begins.

Wringing his hands, he bleats, 'I'm sorry! So dreadfully sorry! It was an accident!'

An accident!?

His lies drip with an oily insincerity that only I can read, for she believes him and forgives him.

I then remember hospital...

Years and years of hospital and being swaddled, head to toe, in bandages. I remember too how my mother, in her floral print

Tattoo thankfully covered.

would come visit. Always with fruit in a crumpled paper bag.

Then, I'd mumble through the bandages, 'I want to go home. Please Mother take me home.'

And she'd hold my hand and sit and cry. I'd watch as her handkerchief became mascara smudged, from dabbing persistently at her eyes.

From time to time she'd be accompanied by Billy. He'd shift awkwardly, conspicuously wouldn't look at me, for he knew what I knew. Then I'd eyeball him, point an accusatory finger, the bandages, however, precluded my intention.

Occasionally, square by square, she'd feed me a half-melted chocolate bar. He'd scold her, announce...

'One must always look after one's teeth!' then proudly clack his.

Afterwards I'd incur the wrath of the nurses, for the chocolate not only stained the bandages, that covered my mouth, it also occasioned me to have bouts of diarr... Or, as they would somewhat indelicately,

Not to mention unprofessionally.

refer to them, 'The Squits'

Then one day, quite out of the blue, it's just Billy who comes to see me. And he no longer shifts awkwardly. In fact he now looks at me triumphantly.

'Where's my Mother?' I mutter.

'Gone...' fingers splaying, as though depicting a puff of smoke.

'When is she coming back?' I say, tears soaking my bandages.

He makes no reply.

And then we go home...

But it's not my home. Not anymore. Just a series of gloomy rooms with dark, heavy curtains (apart from the one with the Venetian Blinds). And it's just me and Billy and those teeth of his. And I shudder as I recall, it wasn't long after that... Clack! He gave me my own teeth.

And then, it begins to fog in again...

Twenty-seven

Its only when the 'fog' lifts, silhouetted against that circular light, that I see him...

Him and his angular face and dark sunken eyes and those teeth of his.

And, as he moves toward me, gives those teeth a … Clack, he pulls an old dental eye mirror down over his left eye. I struggle, for he works his bony fingers deep into my mouth and recoil, back arching, as he finds an exposed nerve.

'I'm sorry! So dreadfully sorry! It was an accident!' his lies still drip with that oily insincerity. 'How many times I told you! One must always look after one's teeth.'

'Lea' me a'one!' my muffled cry.

Meanwhile a door behind him bursts open and he's joined by a huge, slavering… Grizzly Bear!? who makes right for me.

'Who's been eating my porridge?' the bear growls.

Him, and his uniform cap and his yellow oilskins dripping rainwater.

And that's when it occurs to me, I'm still quite delirious.

Twenty-eight

When, just then, my eyes open again...

Only this time, it's just me and Billy and he's still in his scrubs and we're in his small, dark room. The one with the Venetian Blinds. And that's when I find I'm bound hand and foot to, 'Oh no. No!' his fully reclined dentist's chair.

And then, in his left hand, I notice he has a large pair of pliers, which he now begins to tap-tap against my two front teeth. I let out a pitiful 'Unh!' as he has uncovered a problem.

'Aha! Just as I thought suppurative apical periodontitis, left maxillary third molar.'

I shake my head.

'There are treatments, but the immediate course of action would be...?'

'Unh!' I try to speak but his fingers are in my mouth again.

'You're right. It is extraction.' nodding enthusiastically.

'P'ease!' I cry as he reinserts the pliers.

'Okay then. Where is she?'

'Ah 'ont kno...' then, 'Ooh!' as he taps on another nerve.

'You killed her. Didn't you?'

'No!' I cry again. 'I a'ready tol' pol-eece ah 'id'nt... No-ooh!'

Billy, pliers deep in my mouth as can be, shifts position, presses down hard on my left lower jaw…

As my body goes into spasm a pain pulses through me as though I'm electric shocked. And that dull crunch- the one I've just heard- the sound of my tooth imploding.

He stands away then, turning back, proffers a plastic cup. As I'm in no position to take it, he takes my jaw, pours its contents into my mouth, 'Rinse,' he says.

I comply, spitting debris back into the cup.

'Now, what are we going to do with you?' he's enjoying this.

All I can do is shake my head.

'You will tell me, you know.' Then, 'Oh, dear me! Acute alveolar abscess...' and as he gives me his full, undivided attention again, he forces the pliers back into my mouth.

Meanwhile, as tears roll down my cheek, I hear the door open, close again. And then, as Billy turns, I hear him ask…

'How may I help you?'

'That's my line.' she says when… Crack! I hear her pistol.

As Billy gets spun round, he falls onto my legs, says…

'Sorry. So dreadful...'

Then, as he slips onto the tiled floor, it's my turn to sneer. Meanwhile, smoke pluming from her revolver, Dollface, (gun)hand on hip, stands over me. And then I recoil for, in her other hand, I see has a silver, pearl-handled stiletto.

It matches her revolver and mirror.

And now she's running it the length of my right sleeve, rasping it against the threads.

Suddenly her hand drops away and I flinch…

It's only as I look down, I see she's using the knife to cut through my bonds, I want to thank her, but before I can her mouth is on mine, kissing me.

And, as I feel so much better, I don't notice that, she's raising her pistol toward me...

Until that is, that voice is back in my head, telling me, 'Okay Kidder up and at 'em!'

Before I know it...

I'm on my feet, have Dollface pinned against the wall and am relieving her of both pistol and knife.

'You're so tough...' breathy, her lips still on mine.

'Took a class in it,' I, Me Harlow pulling away, training the pistol on her, 'that and French Cuisine.'

'Oh? You should have me over for dinner.'

'Thought I just did.'

'That was starters wait 'til you get to the main...'

'You want dressing with that?'

'Optional. I'd say.'

'Anyway, down to business. Last I remember you were gonna tell me all you know 'bout this Justin character.'

'Do we have to? I'd much rather...' Dollface sashaying forward.

'Ah-ah!' I, Me Harlow in control.

Meanwhile, through the partially open Venetian Blinds, I notice that rolling bank of charcoal cloud and then, and just as I hear that brooding rumble of thunder...

'Fzz!' there's a fork of lightning

And...

'Huh!?' I'm back in front of the bookshop again.

When, just then...

'Fzz!' there's another fork of lightning...

And I'm back in the room. Only now there's no I, Me Harlow. It's just me and Dollface.

'W-Where's Jess?' I say.

Dollface just pouts, sashays forward with that familiar click-clack…

'Oh, won't I do?'

'It's not that… It's just... It's just… Uhm… You're with Justin!... And you keep trying to kill me and... And you're not Jess!'

With my customary, verbal, panache.

Which is when Dollface, clears her throat, pauses a moment and, those blue eyes never leaving me, peels off a pair of fake lashes. Then, pulling a square of cloth from her sleeve she removes that scarlet lipstick of hers, lets the cloth drop. And, as she

Ahem.

pulls back her 'hair', another wave of hair falls across her face... Only now it's crow-black!?

I couldn't be more confused.

'You sure I won't do?' as Dollface pops out a pair of blue contact lenses a pair of big brown eyes become revealed. And that's when I notice her scent...

Her warm, lingering scent.

'Jess?! No, it couldn't... I don't... I don't understand!' I lower my gun.

'Who did you expect? Your Mother?!' then she laughs. And as she laughs there's another rumble of thunder and I notice the bank of charcoal cloud has become whipped into a mass of rolling froth, and the air become charged, crackles with electricity.

And it begins to rain again...

Not just any rain...

When, just then, 'Fzz!' there's another fork of lightning and 'Unh!' it hits me in...

The chest!?

And as I convulse again I notice those smaller forks of lightning shoot from my fingertips and into the ground.

And then, just as that burnt toast smell fills my nose again, I find I'm on my knees again and I'm fading out.

Then in...

And it stays like that until someone, somewhere, finally switches out the lights.

Twenty-nine

Then…

Switches them on again.

When, 'Aah!' I'm back where I started, outside the bookshop, and in my own clothes. As I do a precursory check, I find all my wounds have gone. No bullet hole, no broken tooth, no crab chewed fingers. And he's where he belongs too. 'Cardboard' Harlow. Back behind his bookshop window, hat in place, top lip still curled. And he still leans casually against that stack of books, as if nothing ever happened. Which is when, with that double click from my mouth, I acknowledge him.

It may sound churlish, I'm a little annoyed he doesn't respond.

Then, and as though we're lovers,

Again I may be reading too much into this.

I find I'm in the arms of my lovely policewoman; and who, as before, is all gloves and sharply defined features. As I get to my feet, I see she has her notebook out, I glance down at it.

I was right, her handwriting is impeccable.

'I'm sorry sir but I'm going to have to ask you to…' she says.

Putting a finger to her mouth, I smile at her, 'Later my dear.' For, as I look around, I'm greeted by a sea of anxious gazes from the same gaggle of ghoulish onlookers, all mumbling the same platitudes, but I'm so relieved,

And strangely empowered.

that with a messianic wave I give them all my benediction.

'I console you and preserve you from harm.' when, for the first time in a very long time I laugh heartily. Which, given the circumstances mustn't be deemed appropriate, for some of the crowd step back, others murmur. There is even,

Can you believe it?

some sniggers. And that's when she takes me gently by the arm.

'Sorry sir, I'm going to have to ask you accompany me to the stat…'

'Can't you see my people need me?'

And with that she, talking urgently into her shoulder radio, pulls away. And, as I hear the words…

'Back up required…'

I have already, arms out-splayed, entered the crowd. And they, as I smile my most beatific smile, throng all around me, 'I forgive you… And you… And yes, even you… I forgive all of you.'

Then I hear them, 'Boo!' and 'Hiss!' becoming increasingly hostile, they shout, 'Nut job… Weirdo… Jesus freak!' And that's when they start to push and jostle me. Some even spit.

As she pushes toward me

Now strangely un-empowered.

I say, 'I'm sorry. I don't know what came over me,'

But she's too busy talking into her shoulder to pay me any heed. 'Repeat, back up required!'

And, as she holds them back, I feel bad about leaving her behind.

And then it rains…

Not like before, but still quite heavy.

Meanwhile, I scramble away from the unruly mob, break into a headlong run. Having briefly been the epicentre of a world, I inadvertently created, I glance back only to see it implode behind me.

My heart pounding, like a drum rolling down stairs, I'm convinced the mob are far enough behind and I've run enough. And so, panting, disoriented, soaked to the bone I'm hit with the realization. I still don't know what happened to Jess!

And that's when I decide, I need a drink.

Thirty

I'm not impressed by the first bar I come to. A rundown shack with a neon sign that reads 'The Shady Tree' in red, gothic, lettering. And then there's the metal plaque screwed to the lintel that reads, 'Abandon all hope, ye who enter here…' Nor am I encouraged by its frosted glass front and its depiction of a tree with a hanged man dangling from its branches,

Though on closer inspection it may just be a crack in the glass.

but I go in anyway…

I say go in, I'm now so wet I don't so much enter as pour myself across the threshold. Even after wiping my feet, on the un-welcome mat, I leave a trail of wet behind me. And, as I push my way into the lounge; a dank, dingy hole; little more than a trough with a shabby carpet and cracked plaster walls, I find, judging by the arty clientele that inhabits it, it's curiously popular. If nothing else, it's warm.

Meanwhile, above the hubbub and the beer-glass clattering din, I overhear snatches of frenzied conversation, 'And I'm like, Ohmigod! And he's like 'Relf!' and all over my brand, new rug!'

While elsewhere…

'Course he dumped her, she stubbed a lit cigarette on his neck!'

I find a dark corner, adorned by peeling flock wallpaper, and perch on a badly sprung barstool. As no one seems to be serving I'm almost tempted to help myself. But don't. Instead I wait patiently. And as I wait, a loud tick draws me to an old-fashioned pendulum clock in the corner. As it's hung lopsided, I'm fascinated by just how the pendulum struggles to complete its swing. My reverie, only broken by a song that plays in the back ground. A song that I know
Oh, what is it?…
but can't quite place.

Idly I pick up a coaster, advertising a tropical rum, it shows an indigo ocean lapping a golden shore where a pair of bronzed lovers embrace against a shimmering, orange sun…

Aha!... 'Innocent When You Dream', the song that is.

And, as I get lost in the song, the figures in the coaster becomes Jess and I,

Or is that Jess and me?

either way I bask in the sheer, idyllic bliss of it all, and smile as I look at Jess again. Only it's not Jess anymore. And, as she reaches into her purse, pulls out her gun I see it's Dollfa...

'What can I get you, sir?' he asks.

Him and his jaded demeanour

'Huh!' as I right myself, after nearly falling off the stool. 'B-Brandy, please.' I stutter, transfixed.

'Brandy it is.' he turns away, then back instantly, placing the brandy in front of me. Numb, I reach into my pocket but before I can pay he gets called away.

'What to do!?... Run!'

On my feet, about to do just that, I look down, for my left leg has just become more wet than ever. And that's when I get the pungent smell of fresh...

'Oh no!' as I look up he just stands there, proudly zipping his fly. Even with the nicotine fingers, tumbleweed brows and scarecrow clothes, there's no mistaking him. He didn't need to… Clack! His, now yellow, teeth at me.

But he did.

In an instant I'm off the stool, against the wall, arms flapping like chicken wings. And, as he comes toward me, I let out a whimper.

'You!' he slavers, 'You did this to me!'

'Oh no! Oh, please God no!' I say, wiping his saliva from my cheek.

'And me your father!' he grabs me by my lapels.

'You married my mother, that doesn't make you my father.' Plucking up courage, I grab his wrists.

'You did this to me!' as he shakes his head, looks at his clothes, he cuts a pitiful figure.

'It's nothing compared to what you did to me and…'

Again, uncharacteristically enraged.

'And you killed my Mother!'

'No, I didn't.' as his voice rises, so does his ire, 'It was you! You killed her!'

'No.' I shake my head.

'You did!' he persists, 'She couldn't bear to look at you! Not after…'

'Not after what you did to me!'

'That was an accident!'

Strange as it may seem, I almost believe him.

'You would say that.'

'It was what you became! That's what killed her.'

'No! No! It was you!' I shake my head as I recall that forlorn look she gave me just before she… And then I let go of Billy's wrists.

'It was you.' he says hoarsely.

'No!' I shout, loudly.

Perhaps too loudly.

Then, hard as I can, I push Billy away. Lying sprawled on that shabby carpet, I notice just how pathetic he looks. Which is when the music stops and save for a plink of ice and the tick of the clock, a hush descends…

As everyone stops doing what they're doing and turn to look at me. I manage an, 'Ehm!' then decide I should help Billy up. And as I do I make a sign like it's he who's mad. This doesn't convince anyone.

'It was you all right!' a defiant Billy on his feet pointing an accusing bird claw of a hand at me. 'You killed her!'

Which probably wasn't the most opportune of moments for the

Ahem.

barman to return and, 'Oh, no!' he's accompanied by two policemen. One wearing yellow oilskins while the other is...

Thirty-one

'Fzz!'...

And I'm still yelling 'No!' as I bolt upright, find I'm back outside the bookshop again. Only this time, alone. And, as a stark, silver moon gets buried behind rolling charcoal cloud, I see its night. I don't even check for Harlow. For, now I just want to go home. As I get to my feet I notice it's cold, and so pulling the jacket around me I decide to get a taxi. Which is when, though I hadn't hailed it, one pulls up!?

As a disembodied arm reaches out, the passenger door swings wide. And I get in. When, even before I'm seated... Thunk! The door slams closed behind me.

'The usual?' adjusting his mirror.

'B-But!?' Which is when the chatter returns.

'The Usual!?' How does he know what 'The Usual' is, I'm not sure I know what the usual is? And how does he know where I live? Maybe I've used his cab before? Surely, I'd remember... I'm getting out!

When, just then, the cab pulls away and I get thrown back into the seat.

'The usual it is,' he says and pulls away.

'Yes, yes. The usual.' I nod.

'Seatbelt,' he says.

I comply.

As another feeling of unease takes over me, my only consolation is that hopefully I'm going home. And hopefully Jess will be there. And hopefully I can sleep and wake to find this has all just been one long nightmare...

Hopefully!

I rest my head against the cool, misted glass, close my eyes and concentrate instead on the steady thrum of the engine. When, and just as I manage to block everything out, he starts to mutter in a voice just loud enough for me to hear...

'No one knows how stressful being a taxi driver is.'

It's no joke being a passenger either.

'Staying awake all night...'

I still try to concentrate on the thrum.

'And it's dangerous. You never know what sort of psychopath you could pick up.'

'I'm not one.' I reassure him.

Throwing a sideways glance through the grille, though I can't make out his face, I'm sure he doesn't seem convinced.

'Lucky I can look after myself; and if required I can call on Sammy for back up.'

'Sammy?' not sure I want to ask.

'Meet Sammy.'

Oh no!

He holds up a .45 Colt automatic, so well-oiled even in the dark I see it glint.

Couldn't be the same? Could it? No!

'But you're not going to give me any trouble. Are you?' with a hint of menace.

'Who m-me? N-no!' now even more anxious.

'Relax. I'm just yanking your chain.' he laughs.

'Ha!' I try to laugh back but it dies in my throat.

'Say you wouldn't report me to the police would ya?'

I want to tell him, 'All things considered, it will be quite some time before I'm likely to report anyone to the police.' But, 'No.' comes out instead.

'I mean it's just that there could be a little trouble. What with my license and all...'

Now trying to block him out I've replaced the engines thrum with a, 'Hmm!' as 'Hmm!' my fingers fill my ears.

'I mean; it's not that I don't have a license...'

'Hmm!'

'I do.'

'Hmm!'

'In fact, I have two.'

'Hmm!'

'For the cab and the gun, obviously.'

'Hmm!'

'It's just there might be a slight issue regarding dates...'

'Hmm!'

'Say, what are you doing back there?'

'N-Nothing.' I say 'Hmm!' The more I try to block him out the more I find I can't. It's like he's a transmitter tuned to my frequency.

'You're not some kinda…'

'No, no. I'm not some 'kinda' anything.' I say, 'Hmm!'

'Cos I had me one of them before…'

'Hmm!

'Went all crazy on me he did.'

'Hmm!'

'Sittin' right where you're sittin' now.'

'Hmm!… Hmm!'

' 'course I had to deal with him. Well me and Sammy.'

'Hmm!!… Hmm!!… Hmm!!'

'Least he agreed not to press charges. '

I'm now curled up, foetus-like, trying to put as much distance between him and me as possible. For I can't, 'Hmm!' take much, 'Hmm!' more of this as I, 'Hmm!' feel the headache returning. 'Hmm!' exerting it's vice-like grip. I want him to stop. 'Hmm!' how I want him to 'Hmm!' stop.

When, just then, and just as I begin slapping my forehead again, he, 'Hmm!', does precisely that. For the cab pulls up suddenly and I get catapulted several feet forward only to be caught by the seat belts restraint. When, and with that familiar... Thunk! The door swings open. As I toy with the notion of making a run for it, I remember 'Sammy'.

Peering through the misty glass, I know where we are. Then, undoing my seatbelt, I get out, go to the cab window to pay.

'How much do I owe you?' I say, as 'Fzz!' a fork of lightning licks across the sky, and for a moment, illuminates the interior of the cab...

And that's when I see him. Him and his curled top lip.

'Oh, the usual fee,' he says, 'plus expenses.'

'I-I don't understand.' I say, 'What are you doin-!?'

'I'm on a case.' he says.

'Why the...' I point at the cab.

'I'm undercover. Incognito.'

'W-Who's case are you on?' I ask.

'Yours, Kidder!' then makes that double click sound.

'M-Mine!?' I reel.

'Nearly forgot. You might need this.'

He tosses me 'Sammy' and, as I catch it, it starts to rain again

And not just any rain...

'I'll be seeing you...' he says, still sounds like Abyssinia, 'In Apple Blossom Time!' then as he reverses into the night, switches on the radio. It is,

Needless-to-say...

the 'Gnossienne' that plays.

Thirty-two

And then, as I turn, face Jess' house, the first thing I see is the Mini back in its space.

But how…? Who…?

When just then… Boom! there's a peal of thunder so loud it, ``Bleet-bleet-bleet``, sets off a chorus of house alarms. And, as I make my way toward the door, 'Fzz!' there's another fork of lightning, and that's when the house lights flicker out. Then 'Fzz-fzz! two more forks of lightning, the street-lights do likewise. And then, as the alarms suddenly hush…

All becomes silent, dark, and still.

I check 'Sammy' make sure it's fully loaded. It is. As I approach, I see a key has been left in the lock. And the chatter starts again…

Should I go in? Best not to! Jess might be in there! She might be in danger!… Justin might be in there too!?

Meanwhile, for no other reason than to make the chatter stop, I turn the key…

Thirty-three

As I push open the door, it creaks. 'Anybody there, hello?'

No answer.

Sidling further in I can't decide which is more oppressive, the silence or the dark? Then I detect a movement...

'Jess, that you?' When... Bang! the hall gets lit by muzzle flash as a bullet shatters the mirror behind...

And I see him.

Him and his green paisley.

Instinctively I fire back... And miss for he has scurried upstairs.

Even with that ringing in my ears I hear something being unscrewed and a rattle of tin. As a vision of Justin applying his powder enters my head, I shudder.

'Jess. If you're up there? I'm coming.' My urgent whisper met by his derisive snort.

As the ringing passes I go upstairs. Do so one step at a time. I take the first. Pause. Then the second. As this could take forever I take the remainder, two at a time. When, just as I reach the top, the last step groans underfoot. I pull in tight against the wall and...

Nothing.

From one of the bedrooms I hear shuffling and muffled thumps, as if something, or someone, is getting moved. When, just then, 'Fzz!' the lights flicker back on. And that's when, door slightly ajar, I see into the master bedroom.

What the...!?

For, on one side of a double bed, the body of Young Grim Face is laid out in full Police Dress Uniform. I notice his left arm is outstretched, as though waiting to take someone's hand. When, just then, Justin

And his scars and his big powdery head.

steps from behind the door and fires. And fires again...

As I'm now rolling backwards down stairs, his bullets punch indiscriminate holes into the masonry. Making his way down after me, he's still firing as I roll off the stairs and away. And he keeps firing until… Click-click he's out of bullets. And that's when, running on adrenaline, I'm on my feet, grab the Luger, pull him down the remaining stairs.

'What is going on?' I ask, pointing the .45 at him.

'What is going on?' he just laughs, raises an eyebrow,

Or would do, had he one to raise.

As I press the .45 against his forehead his laughter stops.

'Where's Jess?' I ask.

'Where's Jess?' he laughs again.

'You think you're smarter than me. Don't you?'

'You think you're smarter than me. Don't you?' And then it dawns on me. It's not so much he repeats what I'm saying. More he says what I say, as I say it.

When, 'Fzz!'…

And I'm lying in a bed, looking up a fluorescent lit ceiling. And there's two people standing over me; neither of whose faces I can see.

Then, 'Fzz!'…

I'm back. 'You're playing tricks on me? Aren't you? Stop it!' I say, 'Stop it now!'

He shrugs.

'Have you drugged me!?'

'Even now you still don't see…' he rasps.

'See what!?'

'That I am you.'

'What!?'

'And you, are me.'

'No!' when, just then.

'Fzz!'…

I'm back in that room, strapped to a bed. Looking around, I see all sorts of electrical machinery.

I cry 'No. Please don't!' for I've just seen Ox, and he has just forced a rubber mouth-guard into my mouth. I struggle, but see it's pointless, for not only am I too well restrained, Ox is too big, too strong. And that's when, top lip curled, I see who stands behind him. And, as he reaches toward me, I recoil, for he has just applied what look like electrodes to my forehead. Next, he makes that double click sound. And then, as he presses that button, he says, 'Abyssinia.' And I convulse uncontrollably.

'Fzz!'…

And I'm back again and on impulse, without meaning to… Bang! I've just pulled the trigger. With Justin, now nowhere to be seen, the bullet passes through the door.

For a moment, nothing happens…

Then, as the door creaks open, just a crack. It's Jess' devil key-ring that falls in first. Then, her phone and as I cry, 'Oh, no. No!' Just then, Jess falls through the door. Instinctively I drop to my knees, catch her in my arms, hold her to me, I reassure her, everything will be okay.

But I've seen her wound.

She raises her head, tries to speak.

'Shh, Jess, don't say a word' I'm about to ask, 'What have you done to your hair?' when she starts screaming.

'Wh-Who are you?'

She mustn't be as badly wounded as I thought.

'What are you doing in my house? I'm calling p-police, b-boyfriend is... So 'm I...' And, as she tries to reach for her phone I see it's not Jess. And that's when I recognize her.

Her and her gloves and her sharply defined features.

'Why are you in Jess' house?' I ask, 'Why do you have her keys and phone?' I don't press it as she's in considerable distress. And then I remember Young Grim Face upstairs. And, as the penny drops...

Maybe it's me who's in the wrong house?

She makes one last grab for the phone. I take it off her, tell her...

'I don't want any more police involved, not after the dealings I've had with them.'

'A-Ambulance then...'

Meanwhile I hear that CD player whirr and pause, play that song again.

`` Tell me where your hurting ends and where your fear begins...``

And as I begin to sing it to her, I see that she cries. 'Oh, I'm sorry...' and then I remember, 'Of course. Ambulance! I'm so stupid sometimes.'

'Please hurr-' I pick up her phone and dial. And as I do, she digs her nails deep into me. But by then it's too late. I hold her tight again, try to explain that...

'It's not me you see. It's Justin, he likes to think that he's me. If you saw his face you'd know why.'

And then, 'Fzz!'...

And I see the three nuns are now in the hall too and they've started to sing that song, ''I'm stretched on your grave...''

And then I'm crying as well.

When, 'Fzz!'...

The nuns have gone, and I decide I should go too. But before I do I just want to make sure she's not alone. And so, as I carry her upstairs, we pass the broken mirror. And that's when I see my 'broken' reflection...

Me and my scars and my big powdery head.

Before I place her, hand in hand, with Young Grim Face, I hold her tenderly, tell her, 'I love you.' mean it.

I never said I wasn't fickle.

Then full on the lips, I kiss her. As far as kisses go,

Ever the gentleman.

all I'll say is, it was a cold one.

And then as I hear that commotion, see all those flashing lights, I lay her gently on the bed, linking her hand with Young Grim Face's, when, present company excepted, I realize I'm not alone. For, as the door bursts open, I turn and see him…

Him and his walrus moustache and his yellow slicker dripping rainwater.

As I press against the rain spattered window, he already has his I.D. and service revolver out. I wait for him to smile. He doesn't.

Not even when I say, 'Bad day for it.'

Not even then.

Then, as I hear the hammer being thumbed, see his index finger twitch… Bang!

Aha!

He shoots me in the chest.

'Sammy' still in hand, purely by reflex, I shoot back. And, as he falls to the floor, I crash through the window.

As if I hadn't enough scars!

Ending:

'Unh!' As my, well thumbed, copy of 'Farewell my Lovely' falls to the floor, head pounding, I bolt upright. For, I had the 'dreams' again last night. And, as a paused 'Bogart and Bacall' stare down at me, from the T.V. screen, bracketed securely to the wall, I'm mindful of Poe…

''Is all that we see or seem but a dream within a dream?''

When, just then, the elegant strains of
Needless-to-say.
'The Gnossienne' fill the room.
Or, as it's known around here… Music Therapy.

It's painted a pastel shade of green with matching Velcro curtains and flooring. My room that is. Oh, and my table and chair, also pastel green, including the bolts that secure them to the floor. 'For therapeutic reasons.' Or so the multi-disciplinary team say. But what do they know? It was painted pink before that.
That just drove me mad altogether.

When, and just as I throw back my quilt, the one with the cigarette burns,

I insist they let me smoke.

that LED bulb flashes, followed by the customary ten second pause, as the door to my tiny room slides open.

'Will you walk into my parlour said the spider to the fly 'tis the prettiest little parlour you ever did spy.' I say with an expansive wave as Butler, a male nurse, enters with my medication in a plastic cup. The high dosage of which I hold responsible for those

Oh, so vivid!...

dreams of mine. And my chronic headaches.

It's as though I live with a constant hangover.

'Oh no, no, said the little fly to ask me is in vain, for who goes up your winding stair can ne'er come down again.' with his customary dryness, while his hangdog eyes give him that...

Jaded demeanour.

'You know what day today is?'

'Let me guess. Not my Birthday, nor is it Christmas.' I swallow my meds, along with the spoonful of pro-biotic yoghurt Butler has just handed me. 'My release day?'

'Depot injection day.' placing a blue kidney dish, and the requisite paraphernalia to administer the injection, on a shelf and standing over it.

'Wahay! Two and a half weeks just fly by in here.'

When, just then, the light flashes again and precisely ten seconds later, carrying my breakfast on a tray my

Ahem.

lovely nurse enters. She pauses a moment and purses her lips, for a strand of crow-black hair has just fallen across her face.

'Allow me Jess.' I say, taking the tray from her, putting it on the table.

'That's Nurse Grimason to you.' fixing her hair, she smiles at me.

With those big brown eyes of hers.

'You know I'm quite exhausted Jess. I spent all night looking for you.'

'I told you, I was back on days.'

'That's not what I... Oh, never mind. You know you should give up nursing, become a model.'

'I bet you say that to all the nurses.'

'I don't say it to him.' I point to a nonplussed Butler.

'Tsk! I could never be a model.' she dismisses me, but I've piqued her interest. 'Do you think?'

'Definitely.' I say, 'You're a Dollface!'

While I start my breakfast, a plastic bowl of a something best described as institutional, Butler cracks open a small glass phial, draws a solution up into a syringe. He then shows it to Jess who verifies it against a prescription sheet. I've just finished my breakfast when the light flashes again.

'Ten... Nine... Eight...' I look to my watch. *I'm allowed a plastic, digital one.*

'Aha! Doctor Harlow...' I say.

'What?... Who? You know well my names not Harlow.'

'I presume.'

'That's Doctor Livingstone!'

'Pleased to meet you Doctor Livingstone.'

'No. ''Doctor Livingstone I presume....'' You know Stanley and... Ah, I see another one of your games.' In that glib way of his.

Too glib for my liking.

'Elementary my dear...' I persist.

'Watson?'

'I didn't say anything Father...'

He looks at me bemused.

I feel I owe him an explanation, 'A play on words. Sherlock Holmes. Watson... What son?'

'Ah. I see.' top lip curled as if judging, or mocking, me.

Jess meanwhile, takes me by the arm, leads me back toward the bed. And as I move those little plumes of powder

That cover my glasshouse scars.

spiral toward the fluorescent-lit ceiling. As I pull my green paisley dressing gown around my, shall we say, not inconsiderable girth, I hold it in place, with the scarred fingers of my left hand.

They removed the sash when I was admitted.

Jess and Butler then hold me on the bed, in a way in which I am secure without being restrained, to ensure I don't struggle. I don't usually. Though there was that one time, while administering E.C.T.

I insist on that too.

that they required the services of that orderly. The huge one, with the disfigurement, the one I thought looked like an 'Ox'.

Meanwhile, 'The Good Doctor' makes that, strangely familiar, double click with his mouth as, 'Oof!' he administers the injection into my right…

Ahem.

signs the drug recording sheet and, just as 'Nature boy' plays,

Abyssinia.

is gone.

As I rise from my bed, pulling the dressing gown tight to cover that puckered scar on my chest, I notice the two framed pictures on my bedside locker. The first a group shot of me and 'My Three Singing Angels', the Irish nuns who tended to me on my arrival. While the other is my 'floral print' Mother and me as a child. And I'm holding my red ball. It was taken just before 'The Acci…'

'How about we go for a walk around the grounds after lunch.' Jess, encouragingly.

I look out the reinforced glass window, a progressive psychiatrist had the bars removed, see that it's raining.

And not just any rain…

'No, thanks Jess. Bad day for it.' I say.

'Well it's your decision, but if you change your mind?'

'I won't.'

'If you do,' she persists, 'you know where to find me… Don't you Justin?'

My lovely Jess.

And I smile at her.

If you could call it that?

THE END

Joe would especially like to thank…

Aidan 'Butts' Butler, Doreena Jennings, Pauric Brennan, Aoife and Caroline B'town Office Services, Ferdia MacAnna, Bryan Delaney, Ken Bourke, Padraig Crummy, Eugene McGeehan, Carlow Arts Office, Healys, Meanys, Laharts and Gannons, Parnassus Arts Group, Derek Coyle and all at Carlow Writers Co.Operative…

Oh, and Brigid, Emma and Sarah!

Made in the USA
Middletown, DE
20 March 2019